I0741716

WOMEN and WAR was first produced by Retro Productions at the Spoon Theater, 38 West 38th Street, New York, New York in May of 2010. The performance was directed by Peter Zinn, with sets by Jack and Rebecca Cunningham, costumes by Rebecca Cunningham and Casandera M.J. Lollar, lighting by Justin Sturges, and sound by Jeanne Travis. The production stage manager was Jenny Kennedy. The cast was as follows:

BUDDY, JACK, JOHNNY, VIETNAM MARINE . . . . Lowell Byers

AGNES, GOLD STAR MOTHER, WWII NURSE . . . Heather E. Cunningham

BESTY, DOUGHNUT GAL, MOTHERS OF . . . . Lauren Kelston

HELEN, SP. 4, DELANEY . . . . Casandera M.J. Lollar

CAMP FOLLOWER, HELLO GIRL, WESTERN UNION GIRL,

      VIETNAM NURSE . . . . Elise Rovinsky

WOMEN and WAR
A Reader's Theater Play

by Jack Hilton Cunningham

Baker's Plays
7611 Sunset Blvd.
Los Angeles, CA 90042
bakersplays.com

CHARACTERS

There are five main actors in this play; four women and one man, to play all male roles:

BUDDY & HELEN — a couple in WWII

JOHNNY & AGNES — a couple in the Korean Conflict

JACK & BETSY — a couple in the Vietnam War

VIETNAM MARINE (writes to his mother and brother)

In between the stories of these character's, there are a number of monologues that can be assigned to the four central actresses, or given to new actresses for an expanded casting option. Monologues include:

VIETNAM NURSE

CAMP FOLLOWER

HELLO GIRL

GOLD STAR MOTHER

MOTHERS OF...

WWII NURSE

DOUGHNUT GAL

WESTERN UNION GIRL

SPECIALIST 4TH CLASS DELANEY

If there is a need for even more female characters, additional monologues are included in an appendix.

CAST BREAKDOWN

If the director desires a smaller cast, the breakdown can be as follows:

Actress 1: Camp Follower, Hello Girl, Western Union Girl, Vietnam Nurse

Actress 2: Agnes, Gold Star Mother, WWII Nurse

Actress 3: Betsy, Doughnut Gal, Mothers of...

Actress 4: Helen, Sp. 4 Delaney

Actor 5: Buddy, Johnny, Jack, Vietnam Marine

AUTHOR'S NOTES

The premiere production of *WOMEN and WAR* was presented as a traditional 'reader's theatre' play. Five actors sat in chairs onstage and read from scripts placed on music stands in front of them. Scenery, except for the chairs and music stands, was not required.

Directors of *WOMEN and WAR* are welcome to present this play in the original "reader's theatre" style, but are also welcome to explore various staging styles of their choosing.

The voiceovers and sounds of war should be at a disturbing level at times and other times fade under the actors' voices.

The entire piece should be performed without a break.

EDUCATIONAL GUIDE

An Education Guide by Felicia Lipchik Gell, edited by C. Rebecca Cunningham, written to accompany *WOMEN and WAR* is available in PDF format for producers and educators obtaining rights to perform the play. Please contact Retro Productions at www.retroproductions.org for more information on how to obtain a copy.

To the women in my life:
My Mother
My Wife
My Daughter

PROLOGUE

(As the house lights fade the cast assembles on stage taking their seats as we hear the sound of a radio dial turning into static noise. The sound of static signifies the passing through time when it is heard. The radio dial turns into various archival audio footage of broadcast reporting beginning with 911, Vietnam, Korea, D-Day and WWI.)

[Insert Emily Part I]*

(As the static fades we hear a recording of an instrumental WWII song like Glen Miller's String of Pearls.** *Lights up on Helen and Buddy. The music fades under* **HELEN** *'s first letter.)*

HELEN. Brooklyn, New York, April 1944.

BUDDY. Camp Polk, Louisiana, April 1944.

(Music out.)

HELEN. Darling Buddy,

Got your letter this morning. I was waiting on the stoop when the postman came. I can't seem to do much with my day until I see him coming down the block.

BUDDY. My Dearest Darling Helen,

I started this letter three days ago. I can't seem to put down on this piece of paper that we are shipping out…

---

*This stage direction refers to a monologue included in the appendix section of the play. The choice of whether or not to insert this monologue is up to the director. Other optional monologues are indicated in bold throughout the script.

**Please see Music Use Note on page 3. Please note that this note applies to all Music reference made hereafter.

HELEN. Will you be leaving training camp soon? I hear on the radio that many soldiers are being shipped overseas every day.

(Sounds of WWII prop planes segue into an instrumental in the genre of 1960's music like For What It's Worth. *The music fades beneath the* **VIETNAM MARINE.***)*

VIETNAM MARINE. Danang, Vietnam, May 1968

Dear Ma,

Happy Mother's Day from your son. I've just arrived in Nam to the tune of chopper blades and the fireworks and blare of gunfire. It ain't no Fourth of July celebration, but have no fear, I have both feet on the ground and am surrounded by fellow marines — a great bunch of guys here from all over the states — even a few from good old Philly.

I promise to write as often as I can Ma, but please don't expect too much from me. Ma ya know I wasn't the best student when it came to writing and penmanship; so bear with me.

The chow here is OK Ma, but I sure miss your lasagna. Keep smiling Ma; you'll always be my best girl.

(Instrumental back up, segues into 1940's big band music like String of Pearls *and fades under…)*

HELEN. Brooklyn, April 1944

How is the weather there? It is a lovely spring day here in Brooklyn. Sis and I went to the gardens yesterday and…

(Music out.)

BUDDY. Camp Polk, Louisiana, April 1944

Our shipping orders came Monday. They didn't tell us where we are going or when we will leave, but we're pretty sure we leave Saturday. The orders didn't tell us where we are going. If they would only tell us where we are going. That's the army for you, keep you in suspense and guessing — hurry up and wait — but for what? Just keeping us in suspense.

HELEN. …the grape hyacinths are like a lavender carpet and the tulips, your favorite; seem to be more beautiful this year than ever…

BUDDY. Gosh Sweet Pea, I know this'll as be hard for you to accept as it is for me to write. As miserably hot as it is down here in Louisiana, I would jump at the chance to stay here, but staying in the States has passed me by.

HELEN. … and, my favorite, the daffodils seem to be more spectacular this year. Sis and I walked over to Flatbush Avenue and Prospect Park and sat for a while talking about you and our engagement. Sis seems to think that I should go ahead and start making plans for the wedding, but I said no, I should wait for when you come home. I so want it to be the wedding that the both of us dream of.

BUDDY. On the other hand, Sweet Pea, I feel that your love will be with me wherever they send me.
All my love, Buddy.

HELEN. I love you, Buddy!

(a beat of silence)

CAMP FOLLOWER. My name is Barbara Berry, my friends call me Babs, and I was a "camp follower." Now don't get your drawers in a twist — most people, when they hear the words "camp follower" immediately think of the girls who hung around army camps selling their company to homesick young men. I am not one of those kinda gals. Nope. I am a married woman.
After the president declared war on Germany, Barry, my husband, enlisted and was sent down to Louisiana for basic training, so I took the first bus out of Lawton, Oklahoma to join him.

(sounds of jet planes taking off)

JACK. Vietnam, June 1968
Dear Betsy,
I'm writing this letter to say some things because in this flying business you never know when your next flight will be your last. Please don't think I am being morbid,

but we all have to recognize what is happening here in Vietnam.

I want to be a comfort to you, but the distance separating us makes it very difficult for me to do so. All I can say is that you are in my thoughts during every sortie I fly.

BETSY. Chicago, June 1968

Dear Jack,

Your words make me cry. Being without you this Christmas is going to be difficult. I see you in my teacup in the morning, and in the mirror as I get dressed, and in every young man I see on the street. When I return home, I rush in to pick up your picture from my dresser and hold you in my arms. But Jack, I am so torn by the constant protests that are happening against this war – I know you are doing the right thing over there, but every night when I turn on the television news and I see men burning draft cards, and angry crowds shouting horrible things about our service men, I just don't know which way to turn. Help me to understand Jack.

JACK. Now baby, don't get yourself so upset. I know we are trying to do the right thing over here; all I need to hear is that you are with me in this conflictive, unpopular war. I think I'm strong enough to look past these times of uncertainty as well as to accept my mortality. If my plane does not return tomorrow, I will die without regrets. A little sack time now, must be up first thing tomorrow…

(Music segue.)

CAMP FOLLOWER. Barry met my bus when I arrived in Alexandria, Louisiana. We needed a place for me to stay, so we found ourselves going from house-to-house, knocking on doors. After hours of, "Sorry buddy, but we don't have no spare rooms to rent," we passed a lady and her three young children sitting on a swing in her front yard. When Barry asked her if she had a room to rent, she said she only had four rooms in her house and no inside facilities except running water in the kitchen. But, she said, if that was all right with us, maybe she could put up a bed in the living room. She told us her husband was in the hospital and she needed money to pay the rent and feed the kids. Barry found an old davenport at a used furniture store not far from the house and with the help of some of his army buddies, carried it down the gravel road to the little house.

Later she moved herself into the back bedroom with her three children and rented her bedroom to another couple, Sally and Joe Malone from up north. Mrs. C, as I called her, also allowed us kitchen privileges.

One day Mrs. C told me that her landlord, Mr. Sweeny, gave her notice to vacate the house because she was running a house of ill repute. Well, he put it more bluntly she said, quote, "You and yer kids gotta move, you ain't running no whore house on my property!" So she told me and Sally, "Gals, get your husbands and your marriage licenses ready, we are going to court." Ms. C couldn't afford a lawyer, so she pleaded her case herself, and won!

So we stayed and became known as Mrs. C's "camp followers." Now I tell you, Madam C was a saint to us, and no way was she any other kind of Madam. She took care of me and Sally, and other camp followers when we moved on, like we were her own family.

[Insert Los Alamos Wife Part I]

(Brief battle sounds of Korean Conflict.)

JOHNNY. South Korea, May 1953

Dear Aggie,

The heat is unbearable here in Korea. Pork Chop Hill is no place to spend a warm Sunday afternoon, especially if you don't want to be shot at.

AGNES. Atlanta, May 1953

Dear Johnny,

Grandma Johnson is crazy about Johnny, Jr. She thinks he's getting to look more and more like you all the time. Your mother insists that he takes after me more.

You would be so proud to see how good Junior is while we say the rosary after supper.

JOHNNY. I used to dread those Sunday evening rosaries when I was a boy. We had to keep quiet for too long while the old women, in their black dresses, knelt in front of the crucifix chanting the "Hail Mary," over and over again. Knowing that fresh doughnuts and cold milk would be served afterwards, my impatience always caused some kind of disturbance. Gee, Johnny Junior seems to be following in his dad's footsteps.

(Sounds of war segue into an instrumental in the genre of 1960's music like For What It's Worth. *The music fades beneath the* **VIETNAM NURSE.***)*

VIETNAM NURSE. I had never been away from home before. I was a good Catholic girl and like most Catholic girls, I was only given three professional options — I could join a convent, become a nun, married to the church and live a life of obedience and celibacy — or, option number 2, become a school teacher, teach grammar school, and be a shaper of young minds, or option number three, become a nurse. Well, Florence Nightingale won over Mother Teresa *(a nervous laugh)*. So I became a nurse. A nurse in Vietnam.

My daddy, as I left home, took me in his arms and said, "I raised six kids, five of them boys. Now they are all men, and here I am sending my only little girl off to war." That was the first, and only time I ever saw my daddy cry.

When I got off the plane in Vietnam all I could hear was "Get down, GET DOWN!" I lowered my head and ran as fast as I could — I was there — I was in it — I was a part of it, and it was, and is, a part of me.

(Audible ER noises of generators, respirators, doctors and nurses shouting instructions, etc., build —)

My first day in the OR I looked around at a room filled with rows of beds. Chaos — the smell — the smell, the yelling — nurses yelling, doctors yelling, GI's yelling.

[Insert Emily Part II]

(… and then segue into and 1940's big band song like String of Pearls.*)*

BUDDY. France, July 1944

Dearest Helen,

I can't remember when I wrote ya last, but don't worry I haven't forgotten ya. Your letters give me strength every day, so please keep 'em coming. My outfit has been moving around so much, I haven't had time to write. I am now in the 4th platoon, 3rd squad of company B of the 1st Battalion of the 10th Infantry Regiment of the 5th Division of the 3rd Army. Boy, what a mouthful. Don't forget that I am crazy about you.

(Music out.)

HELEN. Brooklyn, August 1944

My Dear Buddy,

Wow, what an address. I have so much to tell you, but these little V-mail letters just don't give me enough room to let you know how swell you are, and how I pray for your return.

[Insert Los Alamos Wife Part II]

VIETNAM NURSE. I had been an OR nurse in Beaumont, Texas where everything was quiet, sanitized, and orderly; and all of a sudden I found myself surrounded by chaos — filth and screams. On my first day a body was plopped down on a table in front of me — a boy no more than 18 years old — a bloody sheet over his abdomen and I was ordered to "prep" him — that meant clean his wounds, shave him, if necessary, and

"Oh, Yeah!, while you are at it, remove his arm that's just hanging by a piece of loose skin."

I can never clear my mind of the constant whirling of choppers bringing more boys in on more stretchers. We were hit a lot and we had to protect the injured men — one time under a barrage of fire we had to cover the men with mattresses. When there were no more mattresses, I jumped up and covered a boy with my own body — I just jumped on top of him. *(a slight pause)*

There was never a time when you could say, "OK, I'm taking a break — for a smoke — for a drink." Don't even think about a long cool bath, makeup, or having your hair done.

Boys came in all marked up with felt markers with their vital signs written on their bodies and faces *(pause)* like so many tattoos. Our priorities were: first, the worse cases that had a chance of survival, second, the guys who could wait awhile to be patched up, and third, well if death was imminent, then death was allowed to take its course.

(She pauses. More sounds of the O.R.)

When I received my orders to leave Vietnam, I got up, put on a fresh uniform, packed my bags and went over to the OR to say "goodbye." The ventilators were popping — it was hot and smelled of blood, yelling filled the air — it was exactly as it was the day I arrived. Nothing had changed.

(… and again segues into a song)

BUDDY. My dearest Sweet Pea Helen,

(Music out.)

I've made friends with a great bunch of guys and two of 'em are from Brooklyn. One is from Red Hook and the other is from Sheepshead Bay. We talk a lot about the Dodgers, and Ebbets Field. We don't hear much about baseball here so any news you can give us is appreciated. When we win this war, we have agreed to meet at a game and root for the Dodgers. One day they will win the pennant, I just know it.

HELEN. … oh, and honey, your Mom called yesterday to tell me that your Pop went to the game and the Dodgers beat Boston 8 to 7 and the game went to 11 endings.

BUDDY. I haven't had time to write letters to Mom and Pop, so will you please give them my love. These letters are really meant for all the family, as I know ya show every-one all the letters. And sweetheart, it's 'innings' not 'endings'!

Give my best to your Mom and Dad, and to Sis as well.

(Music up, a song like String of Pearls.*)*

HELEN. Lots of kisses darling from all of us.

BUDDY. Love, Buddy.

HELEN. Love, Helen.

(Music out.)

GOLD STAR MOTHER. I belong to the most honorable club in America. The Gold Star Mothers.

MOTHERS OF… My name is Arlene Bishop and I am a disciple of Catherine Curtis and Elizabeth Dilling, founders of the "Mothers Movement," women's war against war.

GOLD STAR MOTHER. When a husband or son is in the war, a banner with a blue star is hung in the window. If he is wounded, a Silver Star is displayed; if he is killed in combat a Gold Star is given to the family to hang in the window so that folks everywhere know the sacrifice that the family has made for our beloved country.

MOTHERS OF… I'm here to rally the women of America who are against this war with our German friends. My aim is to organize as many block groups for the "Mothers Movement" as I can. Show your true stars; join me, and the movement.

GOLD STAR MOTHER. I proudly displayed three blue stars in the window of my modest house in Modesto. Folks would walk by and stop there; some even salute. Passersby always asked if they were for my sons. I stood proudly and I told them, "Yes, my three boys; Joshua, David, and my youngest, Adam."

MOTHERS OF... The Mothers Movement seeks the names of American men who have been killed in the war in Europe. We write to their mothers and tell them "not to be deceived by propaganda into blaming a foreign power" for the death of their sons. Stars hanging in windows signify nothing! It is the President and his war administration that's responsible, not our good friends, the Germans. We endeavor to stop this nonsense of the Allied policy to accept only an unconditional surrender from Germany — that is "un-Christian."

GOLD STAR MOTHER. Slowly my blue stars turned to gold. My baby Adam's star was the first to turn gold, and four weeks later, it was Joshua's. I wrote to my David to cheer him up and told him he's no longer the middle son — he's the only son. David's star turned gold before he received my letter.

MOTHERS OF... Eleanor Roosevelt is a disgrace to this nation. We all know that it's a fact that FDR contracted gonorrhea from Eleanor, who herself had gotten it from a black man. And she is a Jew lover, if not a Jew herself.

GOLD STAR MOTHER. I'm a proud Jewish mother. Folks no longer stop to congratulate me, but to console me. "Chin Up!," I tell them. "What greater sacrifice can a mother make than to give her precious sons for her country?"

MOTHERS OF... There's an octopus trying to foster a Communist takeover of America, and we all know that octopus is the Anti-Defamation League of B'nai B'rith. New York City is the "Jew-Communist" capital of the world. The Jews are the pawns of the Communist movement. Let it be known, they are the reason why American men and boys will never come home again.

GOLD STAR MOTHER. The Gold Star Mothers have a heavy burden to bear. I stand behind our great president in these times of trials and tribulations. He gives me great strength.

MOTHERS OF... I believe in the words of our sister Agnes Waters when she said:

"If we cannot get these traitors out of office by peaceful legal means we can resort to shooting them out! ... Let us demand that this war be stopped at once. Let's keep a clothesline handy in every little back yard to hang the traitors, or a gun!"*

GOLD STAR MOTHER. My boys never left me — I still see them every day. Climbing that big tree in the back yard, scraping a knee while skating, chasing the cat and running after the dog, collecting cans and newspapers for the war effort. Before they left they planted a Victory Garden and gave me strict instructions on how to keep it growing. Giving up a son is the hardest part of being a mother; losing a son to war is the agony of motherhood. No more will I call up the stairs to them — no more will I sit up at night worrying when they come home late — no more will I fall fast asleep in peace when I hear the key in the door — no more — no more.

[Insert Emily Part II]

(*More radio search noises, a clip from* **MA PERKINS,** *and then noises of crowds and airplanes crashing and an announcer:*)

(*A voice announcing the 9/11 disaster.*)

(*More crashing noises fading under a current hip-hop song.*)

---

* *[This quote is taken from an article published in 1944 in "Women's Home Companion" magazine and printed on page 338 of "Our Mothers' War" by Emily Yellin, published by Free Press, New York City, NY, ISBN 0-7432-4516-4 (Pbk).]*

SPECIALIST FOURTH CLASS DELANEY. I was seventeen when 9/11 happened. I woke up that morning to Mamma making breakfast — the smells of bacon frying and coffee brewing — smells that I will forever associate with that morning — Mamma never made breakfast on a workday before. But that morning the television in the living room was blaring reports of airplanes crashing into buildings in New York City.

That morning I told my Mom and Dad that I was going to do my part to help see that this horrible thing never happened again to our country. I joined my high school's ROTC. After graduating the following May, I joined the Army.

(Instead of static we hear a steady tone as the dial is being searched for news of the war. More static and searching and it comes to a song like For What It's Worth, *the song fades under.)*

VIETNAM MARINE. Nam, January 1968

Dear Ma,

Tet is no holiday. It leaves little time to write to you. The American casualties they say is about 2,500, but they are saying the Vietcong lost up to 37,00 troops, but they still keep coming at us.

I am tired and weary Mom, but I gotta keep plodding on and dreaming of your manicotti!

Love ya' Ma.

(Sounds of choppers fade in the distance and we hear pastoral sounds, a gentle breeze in trees, birds, etc., then more radio static sounds, and we hear a few bars of a WWI song like Over There *that fades into sounds of telephone operators some speaking French, others English.)*

HELLO GIRL. *(She speaks with a slight French accent.)* It was bitter cold the day when I landed in France in 1918 — a day that was much like many days in Bangor, Maine. I was an operator for the telephone company in Bangor when I heard that the Army was looking for switch-board operators who spoke French. I was one of 223 girls who would be shipped to France. We were sworn into the U.S. Army Signal Corps Telephone Units as soldiers. Think of that, the first women to serve in the Army and yet, at home we didn't have the right to vote.

BUDDY. France, November 1944

My dear Helen,

I yearn for you and a warm sunny day in Brooklyn. I have never been so cold in all my life. Although I have plenty of clothes to keep me warm, my feet still get cold. I am wearing two pairs of wool socks and they make my boots so tight that I can't wiggle my toes.

HELEN. This little piggy went to market — darling keep those toes warm, you will need all 10 when you get home to walk me down the aisle, and then to keep my feet warm every night. I yearn for you Buddy Boy...

BUDDY. ...oh, how I long to come home.

HELEN. ...come home, oh Buddy Boy, come home.

HELLO GIRL. After arriving in France I was assigned to a station in Chaumont. The work was hard. Sometimes the noises of war made it difficult to hear voices from the other end of the line. We had to scream at the top of our lungs in order to be heard through the telephone lines — all the girls screaming into their instruments at the same time. I knew I was doing something impor-tant — the excitement — the constant noise kept me going.

I was sent from Chaumont to Souilly to reinforce the girls there. Conditions were awful. The weather was cold and it rained constantly. There was mud every-where. The bottom of my skirt and my boots were caked with mud. The morning of November 11th, 1918 the hello girls handled heavier than usual voice traffic. Gradually the noises of war ceased. I remember that day well; it was another blustery cold day in November. When the "hello girls" returned to the States we were

told that we were no longer "sworn in" members of
the Army. After failing to persuade Congress in 1930
to recognize us as full-fledged members of the military, more than fifty bills granting veteran status to the
"hello girls" were introduced in Congress. Finally, in
1978 we succeeded. Congress passed a bill to recognize
the 223 women as veterans. Only a handful of us were
still alive.

(A few bars of a WWI song segues into a holiday tune.)

BUDDY. France, Christmas Eve, 1944
Helen, my darling,

(Music out.)

My days are bluer than ever, and when I think of you,
I have to fight back the tears so my buddies won't see.
All of us guys left in Company B sit around in our
dirty uniforms, heavy boots, and heavy hearts, and sing
"Peace on Earth, Good Will to Men." We try our best
to comfort each other.

HELEN. Brooklyn, Christmas Day, 1944
Sweet, sweet Buddy,
Mr. Berlin hit it right this year. We don't have to dream;
we have a white Christmas. I woke up this morning and
looked outside to a glorious day. I was elated, but only
for a moment, and then I prayed this will be the last
Christmas we spend apart. I lit a candle for you this
morning at mass and said a special prayer for you.

BUDDY. Love you …

HELEN. Love you …

[Insert Axis Sally]

(We hear a few more bars of a song like White
Christmas*)*

JOHNNY. Somewhere in Korea, January 1954
Dearest Agnes,

(Music out.)

I received the pictures you sent. They are swell. Johnny, Jr. is cute in his cowboy suit. He sure is a show off, just like his old man. When I get home you can look forward to more babies and that little house with a white picket fence and a dog.

AGNES. Atlanta, February 1954

I met Sally Bergstrum this morning after Mass and she was asking after you. Charlie is still in Japan for R&R, she thinks. She hasn't heard from him in weeks. Do you have any news about what's happening with his outfit?

JOHNNY. I had some well-earned R&R in Japan last week, too. I hope you got the postcards I sent. Having a week to do almost nothing found me with lots of time on my hands. What else is a married guy to do? The single guys, well that's another story. I asked around about Charlie Bergstrum, but no one seemed to know. One guy said that he heard Charlie might be missing in action, but can't say for sure. I know this isn't any help so don't tell Sally. I'm sure she probably knows about him by now anyway, if he is OK.

AGNES. Dear Johnny,

I am so glad you had some free time. We all loved the postcards. The one of the Geisha gave me cause for concern *(chuckle).* That was just a picture and not someone you might have, well you know what I am trying to say.

I love you, Johnny Johnson, Junior says "I love you, Daddy."

(We hear more choppers that segue into a song like String of Pearls *under the next Buddy/Helen sequence.)*

BUDDY. Somewhere in France, January, 1945

Christmas and New Year's were just two more days for us. The weather is rotten. Wish I had some good news to send, Sweet Pea, but I don't.

HELEN. My Darling,

(Music out.)

Missing you is so painful. It helps if I try to keep busy. Do you remember my high school friend Rachel? I met her the other day at Abraham & Strauss and we went over to Schraffs for a soda, and we talked for a very long while. She said that being a Jewish wife in Brooklyn has been very difficult. There is so much hatred toward the Jews she sometimes thinks that her parents might as well have stayed in Poland and suffered the oppression that is open rather than suffer the sneers and whispers that she feels whenever she walks down Flatbush Avenue.

My darling, I am trying so hard to be a good American and do my part. I got a job down at the navy yards and I encouraged Rachel to do the same; it's hard work, but I don't complain. Women all over this country are going to work and keeping house and being mothers and feeding their families even with the rations of sugar and butter. Last week there was no butter to be had so we bought oleomargarine, it comes in a block, white as lard, with a little packet of yellow coloring that you mix with the oleo till it looks like butter. But it tastes like lard.

BUDDY. Sugar, you are sugar enough for me. Keep your head high and never lose that beautiful smile that I fell in love with. Yes, I remember your friend Rachel, and the next time you see her please tell her to keep her chin up and not give up hope. I pray that when this war is over, and I am back home again, that will be the end of hatred and we will all live as free Americans and worship in our own way, Jews and Christians alike. Don't worry about the butter, or me, I will butter you up when I get back to Brooklyn!

HELEN. Buddy Dear,

When I get home at night my muscles ache with pain. Things are surely getting worse here in Brooklyn. I received a new book of ration stamps today, which was a relief. Mom and Dad are helping out as much as they can by standing in line when food is available. We just keep tightening our belts and making do with less and less.

I love you.

BUDDY. I love you.

(Some static and more dial searching and we hear a bit of a military song like Praise the Lord and Pass the Ammunition *as it fades under* **WWII NURSE.***)*

WWII NURSE. Ah, you bet'cha.

I grew up in a large family in a small town south of the twin cities. My dream was to become a nurse, so after graduating high school I attended a nursing program at our junior college. Papa worked in the General Mills plant and Mama kept house. We weren't rich, but we weren't poor either. Having many brothers and sisters kept us all busy looking out for each other; when one got the measles we all got the measles; when one brought home the mumps, we all had the mumps. I guess that's why I am a nurse.

When two of my brothers joined the navy, I wanted to do my part as well. After all, why should we leave it to only the men to carry the burden of war? So I enlisted in the Navy and was sent to the Pacific — Corregidor, Bataan, Guam, and Saipan. The hospital ships are always short staffed and filled with the wounded — our boys with limbs blown off, faces scarred for life; boys barely able to assist themselves on crutches, battlefield bandages barely holding their mangled bodies together. They all seem to be so lonely and homesick. More often than not, they just want to talk to someone. They show me pictures of their wives, moms, and girls from back in the States. After my official daily tour, I write letters for the boys without hands or arms or who were so badly burned that they cannot hold a pen to write. Many nights I become the messenger of news like, "gee Mom, my right arm is missing in action," or "dear Sally, guess what, I will no longer be able to play football, which you hate, because I am now missing both legs." It is difficult to write these things on paper and difficult for me not to cry along with them. I slip away to cry alone, I'd never let the boys see me cry, they never see me cry.

(A beat of silence allowing the mood to change. If there is a change of light it should go brighter for **DOUGHNUT GAL.***)*

DOUGHNUT GAL. I know you've heard of the USO Girls who toured behind the lines to entertain the troops. Well, I was a Doughnut Gal, one of the gals that drove two-ton army trucks and served doughnuts and hot steaming coffee to the men. Well, I called myself a Doughnut Gal. Molly is my name. From down south Alabama.

Alice, my doughnut companion, and me ended up somewhere in France to serve our boys hot coffee and doughnuts. So, me and Alice would load our old truck with sacks of flour, sugar and coffee, and cans of cooking oil, and hit the road by five every morning. What a bumpy ride! By the end of the day we were as greasy as the doughnuts. No need for any beauty lotions for our hair, the oil kept it preee-ty shiny. After a day 'on the range', our blouses and skirts needed degreasing as well.

Did you know that a greater percentage of Doughnut Gals were killed in action in the European Theater than gals from any of the other women's services? Put that in your record book, Uncle Sam!

In 1945 Alice and I split up; she was sent to Le Harve, and I, well lucky me, I was sent to England where my doughnut days continued and my jitterbugging days began. There was this very large, empty warehouse building where the boys assembled for their next assignments. There was lots of music, and the boys loved to jitterbug, and since I knew a few steps — move over English gals — I went from being just a 'Doughnut Gal' to a 'jitterbug gal'. Give 'em some hot coffee and doughnuts, and jitter they would. And oh boy, could those boys jitterbug!

(We hear a bar or two of a 1950's song like Wayward Wind.*)*

JOHNNY. Korea, April 1954

Dear Aggie and Little Johnny,

(Music out.)

I can't explain why I have not been writing more. But you see, here in this mess, there is not a solider with a rifle that knows which way to point. We hear the enemy fire, we see the tracers light up the sky, and some times we are just lucky, like the other day when we captured those North Koreans.

AGNES. Atlanta, April 1954

Dear Johnny:

I let your Mom and Dad read the 10-page letter you wrote. You should have seen your Dad's face when he read about the 28 prisoners you captured. That was something else for him to brag about. Grandma Johnson laughed and told us you're doing a whole lot more than your father did when he was in the army.

You're so thoughtful, honey. That's one of the many, many things I love so much about you, Johnny darling. There isn't any more news so I'll close for now.

JOHNNY. This morning we encountered, face-to-face, a team of North Koreans. They were lobbing grenades and firing at us, and as they charged toward us I fired and hit one in the face. I watched as he fell silent and died almost instantly. Agnes, I can't tell you how awful I feel to have killed another man. I immediately asked God to forgive me, and oh Agnes, please forgive me as well. I am so confused. I will go to confession the first chance I get.

AGNES. We put little Johnny in Kindergarten this week. I do believe it was harder on me to leave him, than it was for him on the first day. He seems to be having a wonderful time with the other boys and girls and is learning his numbers and alphabet so fast.

Oh, Johnny, I pray that when this war is over there will be no more wars, so little Johnny and all the boys and girls can grow up in a world of peace and freedom. I know that day will come, Johnny, and I am doing my part to see that it does.

(Sounds of Korean War segue into sounds of WWII.)

BUDDY. France, February, 1945

My darling,

I attended Mass this morning. Today we were near this little bombed out town and came upon a small church that was still standing. There is a hole in the roof and everything was a bit tattered and soaked. I felt so much closer to God just being in a church again. The sun came out strong just as the service began and a shaft of bright sunlight came through the broken roof and fell upon the altar. It was as if God was telling us He is on our side. We sure were a happy bunch of worn out Catholics. We move out in the morning, going north into Kraut-land. Pray for us.

HELEN. I am doing my best to keep up my spirits. I went to confession yesterday, and Father Malone asked about you. We walked down the aisle and chatted for quite a while. The church is a great comfort to me and keeps me believing in a wonderful future ahead of us when you return home.

Buddy, I love you.

BUDDY. I love you Helen.

BETSY. I love you Jack

JACK. I love you Betsy.

AGNES. I love you Johnny

JOHNNY. I love you Agnes.

(More sounds of war.)

WWII NURSE. Today we had a new shipment of wounded, and we had to undress men who had not bathed in months. There is no modesty, but only looks of thanks. One soldier looked up at me as I was sponging him and said, "I prayed last night that I could bathe one more time before I die." He stopped breathing — but I continued to bathe him until another nurse tapped me on the shoulder and said, "Honey, he's gone; you can stop now."

(The lights dim on all the women as they bow their heads and hold hands. Their actions should reflect a solemn hippie "Sit-in" as we see a man pass in front of the women in full military fashion imitating a funeral march. We hear the sound of the iron Victory Bell ringing in the distance from the Kent State campus bell tower as the following archival sound recordings play: A press conference held by Ohio Gov. James Rhodes "We're going to use every part of the law enforcement agency of Ohio to drive them out of Kent. We are going to eradicate the problem not treat the symptom." and forensic audio footage of M1 Garand rifles being fired by the National Guard on the Vietnam protesters. The lights slowly fade up as we hear the voices of the war protesters yelling "Hell No! We won't go!")

VIETNAM MARINE. Tay Ninh Province, Nam, October, 1968
Little Brother,

(Sound out.)

Take this advice from me. Stay as far away as you can from the fucking army and this shit-hole called Nam. Trust me, being a grunt in this godforsaken country ain't no fun. Don't be like me, go to college and get good grades or burn your draft card and head straight to Canada. Do this one thing for me, brother. And if I ever get home, I promise to be the big brother that I never was before. And, oh yeah, give Ma a big kiss for the both of us.

I never said this before, but I love you kid.

Your Big Brother

AGNES. Johnny Jr. is so much like you Johnny, more and more each day, I see you in him. Even your mother is beginning to see you in the way he walks across the floor and turns and looks at us with those big brown eyes. She sings him a song that she said she used to sing to you. Do you remember it, Johnny? It goes something like this: "Oh, Johnny, Oh, Johnny, how you can love, Oh, Johnny, Oh, Johnny, heaven above."

JOHNNY. I used to get so embarrassed when she sang that song and my friends were there. But now that I think back, it was such an endearing thing that she did. I know she loved me more than anything. Since I was an only child, she had lots of love to give. Our little Johnny must have brothers and sisters. And I'll see to that when I get home, so prepare yourself, Aggie. Prepare yourself! And Aggie, not to worry, but I took some serious shrapnel in my right thigh, but the medics tell me everything is going to be A-OK.
Love, Johnny

AGNES. Oh, Johnny, are you hurt bad? Johnny, I do worry. Promise me Johnny that you are A-OK and that I need not worry.
I love you Johnny.

(A beat of silence… and we hear Korean war sounds that segue into WWII war sounds.)

HELEN. Brooklyn, April, 1945
Dear Buddy,
Not hearing from you is agonizing. The radio and newspapers tell us that the Germans are in retreat and that our Allied forces are advancing to end this terrible war. I light a candle for you every day at St. Dominics on my way to work. I pray every day that you are safe and will come home soon.

BUDDY. Germany, May, 1945
My dearest Helen,
I know you are worried since you haven't heard from me in months. As we crossed the border into Germany, we were ambushed and taken prisoner. It has been hell

not knowing what was happening in the war for these many months. We were not allowed to send or receive mail. Then our prayers were answered, and the allied forces arrived.

What a sight! Men, hundreds of us, falling to our knees to pray as we watched the Star Spangled Banner, Old Glory, rise over this 'pit of hell' we have called home these many months.

HELEN. We are getting lots of reports of the thousands of Jews that were sent to labor camps and then murdered in the gas chambers in Germany and Poland. Can it all be true? When will you be coming home Buddy? Now that it is over, over there.

BUDDY. Yep, the war in Europe is over. We hear the reports daily, and it sounds too good to be true. We smile, but there is no jump for joy; we are just too tired. Rest is what we need, just some quiet moments with time to forget ...

(We hear a song like Kate Smith singing God Bless America *and it fades under...)*

I'm coming home Sweet Pea, hold your breath, I will be Brooklyn bound on the USNS Buckner, a trusted old tub that will take me across the north Atlantic and into your arms.

(Music out.)

HELEN. Oh, my Buddy, I am checking the papers every day to see when the Buckner docks here in Brooklyn. I'll be wearing my daffodil-yellow dress and waving the good old Red, White and Blue. Oh Buddy, you are coming home!

(Music fades under Western Union Girl.)

WESTERN UNION GIRL. Sometimes I come to the icebox, open the door, and just stand here, wondering what it was that I came here for. Memory is a funny thing at my age. "Madge McAlister," I say to myself, "what's come over you?" Then I hear the tick-tock-tick of the old regulator in the hall, and I am back one day in June, 1944.

(Music out.)

After high school most of the boys of Baylor went right to work in the mills or on their family's farm; few if any, ever went to college. So for a few extra dollars they joined the National Guard and spent one night a month playing soldier. Aaron, my older brother, joined the Guard as soon as he was old enough. When the war began in Europe, his entire unit was called into active duty.

I worked as the Western Union Girl in Baylor, Kentucky and it was my job each morning to turn the Teletype machine on and connect with Lexington.

It was June 6, 1944 when our boys were sent to that beach in France the army called Omaha. Heroes all, over 10,000 lost their lives and were buried on the bluff overlooking the sea.

On that morning in June I switched on the teletype machine, and when it warmed up I typed "Good Morning, Lexington, go ahead." And the reply came, "Good Morning Baylor. We have casualties." The machine began to sputter and click-click-click, shooting out tape faster than I had ever seen before.

Click-click-click, the tape just kept coming. I did my best to put the tape in the tank of water, and with my thimble and ruler stripped it onto the yellow Western Union stationary. "The Secretary of War desires me to express my feeling of regret ..." click-click-click. Another yellow piece of paper, another regret, another name, another address. I pasted and I pasted. Click-click-click "regret" John Seers, click "regret" Albert Staulings, click "regret" Andy Barrow, click-click-click.

My younger brother, Billy, leaned his old Montgomery-Ward bicycle against the fire hydrant in front of the office that morning. Billy delivered the telegrams whenever there was one. That day there was more than a young boy on his bike could handle. So I called Sheriff McCoy to say that I needed help. He organized a group of local men with cars or trucks to deliver the telegrams. Click-click-click "regrets" Bobby Barnes, "regrets" Dudley Dickerson, "regrets" Larry Holloway … click-click-click.

All in all, there were more telegrams than I can remember. As lunchtime approached I was pretty much in a daze and then … click-click-click … "It is with profound regret that I … click … Aaron MacAlister" … my dear brother …

In 1994 on the fiftieth anniversary of D-Day, I went to France and among the rows and rows of white marble crosses, on a bluff overlooking the sea, I found my beloved brother, Aaron.

(She turns away from audience, and then turns back.)

Now, what was it that I came to the icebox for? Oh yeah, the milk.

(A few more bars of a war song like Praise the Lord and Pass the ammunition *and it segues into a current rap, fade under.)*

SPECIALIST FOURTH CLASS DELANEY. After my basic training I served a tour in Afghanistan in a non-combat situation. Women weren't allowed in combat roles, and still ain't. I was serving over there when my truck was hit. Three soldiers was killed and I was seriously wounded. When I woke up I discovered that my legs was so badly damaged that both of 'em had to be amputated just under the knees. I survived, as you can see, and with my prosthesis I can walk as normal as any other of you here. Well, the downer is that I can't dance no more, can't wear skirts or dresses, just pants for me now — but that's cool; I can deal with that.

BETSY. Chicago, July, 1968

Dear Jack:

Well, the boys are off in every direction these days. Bruce is in the Boy Scouts now, Paul is playing Little League, and Hank has taken an interest in girls. I have a new job — taxi driver. The Chevy station wagon is holding on by gosh and by golly, and I hold my breath every time there is distance to travel with the boys. Hank got his driver's license yesterday, so now I have another reason to worry. My men; they will be the death of me yet!

JACK. Vietnam, August 1968

Betsy dear,

I have been thinking and if anything happens to me, don't let the memories of me keep you from marrying again. The boys will need a good father and you deserve a good husband. I just don't want you to be alone. Life should be lived to the fullest. Go for it girl — live life, that's what it is for.

BETSY. Now Jack, there is no need to talk like that. I believe that you will be resuming your fatherly and husbandly duties before long.

JACK. Keep on smiling, put on some makeup, buy yourself a new dress, give the boys a hug, and some discipline when needed, and pave the road of your life for new adventures. If I cannot share those adventures with you, then just remember me every now and then — not too often, or it'll cramp your style, you know — and as long as I'm remembered, I'll not really be dead. I'll still be around in Bruce, Paul, and Hank.

Love you Betsy, Jack

BETSY. Now Jack, you shouldn't go on and on like that. I will not consider your not returning home, not for one second. You will come home Jack, I know you will. I do plan on buying a new dress, and I'll have the boys all starched and ironed and standing at attention when you walk up that walk and into my arms.

The boys send their love,

Betsy

HELEN. Dear Friends,

My Buddy is home! And you are all invited to celebrate the nuptials of Helen Sullivan and Buddy Brugaletta at St. Dominic's Church on Flatbush Avenue in Brooklyn, on the 5th Day of October, 1945.

A reception will follow in the church hall.

(Sounds of a jet fighter plane taking off in the distance.)

BETSY. Chicago, September 1968

Dear Jack,

It has been a week since your last letter. I hope and pray that you are just so busy flying sorties that you haven't had the time to write. Hank had his first date last night; I drove him and his girl to the movies. I sat in the back of the theatre; they sat up front. The movie was "The Creation of the Humanoids" — now don't laugh because I sat through the whole thing thinking all the time that I was doing it for you. I dropped them off at Bloomfields for ice cream sodas, came home, had a cup of coffee and finished my turn as chauffeur by dropping Hank's girl at her house. Hank walked her to her door — you would have been proud. I guess our boys are growing up. Time for bed. I'll write again soon.

Betsy.

(Chopper sounds fade into intro of a current war song like For What It's Worth *and song fades under Vietnam Marine.)*

VIETNAM MARINE. My Ma makes the best meatballs in all of Philadelphia. Boy, can my Ma cook. Ain't tasted that kinda cooking since I can't remember. Sometimes I just close my eyes and inhale, trying to remember the sweet smells of sweet green peppers and sausages frying in the pan. "Mangia" Ma always says, "Mangia, Arnie, so you can grow up to be a soldier like your Uncle Joey in World War II."

Yesterday we went up the delta toward Cambodia. Our line of troops hit a snag. There was this gang of gooks waiting for us in the rice paddies. They eat a lot of rice here in these parts, not like us Italians — we eat pasta, spaghetti, macaroni, lasagna, tortellini, and spinach ravioli — Ma I know you made them, just to get me to eat my spinach. *(He pauses briefly.)* We were hit by enemy fire, and I saw my Sarge get hit — blood all over the place — he fell in front of me chokin' and spittin' blood. I tried to stop the bleeding, but I couldn't. He died in my arms. The next thing I knew two more of my buddies were hit. Private Lars Johnson was lying on his back with his blond curly hair all sticky with blood and mud, looking up at me with those big, blue Scandinavian eyes. A blank stare. Another son dead; another Ma mourning.

All of a sudden there was the loudest explosion I have ever heard inside my head — and all of the noises of war, the grenades, the copters overhead, the explosions, the shouts of pain and cries for help — all washed away into silence — sweet silence.

The fog cleared and everything was peaceful — just like eating your tiramisu, Ma — food I'll share with the angels.

Ma, don't cry.

(After a beat of total silence a bar or two of a song like For What It's Worth *are heard again and segues into chopper noises and an announcer:* "...April 30, 1975 – Today at 8:35 a.m., North Vietnamese troops are pouring into Saigon with little resistance. The war, that has taken so many of our brave American men and women, is now over. ..." *Chopper noises fade.)*

BETSY. Chicago, October, 1968

Dear Jack:

It has been three weeks now and no word from you. The boys and I are beginning to worry. Please just send a card to let us know that you are OK. Everything is good here. I bought that new dress today. The boys said I looked more like Lady Bird than Jackie-O. I was impressed that they even noticed. I guess I am getting older, I know this waiting is taking its toll on me, but I keep smiling.

(We hear radio static once again, and, "... President Eisenhower announced today that an accord has been reached in the Korean conflict; a demilitarized zone has been established at the 38th parallel." We hear sounds of helicopters in the foreground and bursts of fire in the background and more rap.)

SPECIALIST FOURTH CLASS DELANEY. I suffer from what they call post-traumatic stress disorder. When I started therapy it seemed to me that my symptoms was only caused because I lost my legs. I don't remember nothing — I might have passed out — I don't know — but I do remember that everything went dark and the smell of smoke and burning flesh returns to me in an instant sometimes, especially, if I smell bacon cooking or coffee brewing. After all I had been the victim of a terrorist attack on my unit and three of my fellow soldiers was killed — two men and one woman. Did you know that one out of every ten people serving in the armed forces today is a woman and I read somewhere that over 220,000 or 11 percent of troops sent to Afghanistan and Iraq were women? In the Vietnam War the percentage of women to men was much, much smaller and almost all of them women was nurses. Not so in today's army. One day in Afghanistan I overheard a conversation between three soldiers and the first soldier said, "women in the army are just whores," and the second one said, "yeah, or bitches," and the third one joined in and said, "nah, most of 'em are dykes — just try fucking one, they gotta be lesbos." Now there's a large number of soldiers that don't think of the women as "sisters, wives or sweethearts," they think of 'em as "whores, bitches, or dykes." I was told that in Vietnam there were Asian whorehouses set up by governments, supported by the USA, as R&R areas for the service men to relieve their sexual desires, or I think they put it as their "sexual needs". Well, not so in Afghanistan or Iraq, there are no whorehouses, no brothels, no bordellos — but there are plenty of female service personnel. So some of the men think that women soldiers are there just to have sex with 'em.

BETSY. Chicago, November, 1968

Dear Jack,

They must be keeping you very busy my darling. Not a word in a very long time. I am holding up OK by propping myself against every doorway I attempt to go through. Not hearing from you is exhausting.

Mom and Dad are planning to visit for Thanksgiving. So I guess I will be cooking that turkey after all. There will be fresh baked rolls, and pies coming out of the oven until we collapse from the sheer joy of cooking.

Now that I have your mouth watering, I'll close for now — just wishing you will be with us for Thanksgiving.

Betsy.

SPECIALIST FOURTH CLASS DELANEY. I ain't condemning all the men who serve their country honorably, but the percentage that takes advantage of their female counterparts is greater than the numbers say. It wasn't until my therapist began to help me dig into my short military career that I was able to admit that. This ain't easy to talk about, but my therapist tells me I gotta, cause I can't let go of the anger, but — well here it is, and I swear this on my Grandmama's grave — I was raped when I was in Afghanistan. And I heard stories from other girls about being raped too. When I was in Afghanistan I was raped by my first lieutenant. Because I was only an enlisted soldier, I was afraid that if I reported it, I wouldn't be believed. He was handsome, a very popular officer amongst the troops, so who would believe that I hadn't agreed to have sex with him? A girlfriend of mine was assaulted in Iraq. It was by a gang of three soldiers; all enlisted men. They got her drunk, and, well you can probably guess the rest. She filed charges, but they were dismissed due to lack of evidence. The three soldiers that she identified as her attackers were given letters of admonishment. *(She gestures in amazement.)* End of story! Hummmph!

JOHNNY. San Francisco, August 1954

Dear Aggie,

Here I am again on the good old U.S. of A. soil — it feels so good under my foot. Yes, I said foot — the shrapnel lodged in my right thigh was more serious than I told you and my right leg was amputated. I hobble OK on one leg and one crutch. I'm sure Junior will have a field day teasing the "old man" as the "old gimp" now. I will get my final discharge papers tomorrow, honorable at that, and will be flying to Atlanta as soon as I can get out of here. It's going to be a new and different life, Aggie; so keep smiling, we are going to be just fine.

I love you and need you more than ever …

AGNES. Oh Johnny, Johnny Jr. is jumping for joy and all I can do is sing: Oh Johnny, Oh Johnny heavens above …"

(As she signs the song segues into a recording of Oh Johnny.*)*

[Insert Three Soldiers Letters to Their Moms]

BETSY. December, 1968 STOP Mom and Dad STOP The dreaded doorbell rang yesterday STOP Two young officers came to inform me that Jack is dead STOP At first they thought he was shot down and taken prisoner, but later learned that he had not survived STOP. His body will arrive in California next week STOP I am holding up as well as one can expect STOP The boys are a great comfort to me STOP Please come STOP Betsy.

(Sounds of missiles being fired and distant explosions fade under a female voice recording of a verse of a current song like How Did I Get Here ... *fades under below.)*

SPECIALIST FOURTH CLASS DELANEY. It's been nine years since 9/11. I am 26 years old, but I feel oh, so much older. How did I get here? Well, let me tell you — this is my story, but I am sure there are many, many more women with stories just like mine. Even though women are assigned non-combat duties in Afghanistan and Iraq, the lines between combat and non-combat are so blurry that all service personnel are in danger, and not just the men who are quote, doing the fightin', unquote. We serve; we are abused; we come home — we fight the demons.

I may not be able to dance no more, not with these plastic legs, but that's cool, I can live with that. But will I ever be able to trust other men? Fall in love? Shit, have a normal sex life, get married and have children? Right now I ain't seein' that happening. I have heard of a program in California that is just for women who are diagnosed with PTSD *(she pauses),* maybe I'll go there...

WESTERN UNION GIRL. ... on the fiftieth anniversary of D-Day, I went to France and on a bluff, overlooking the sea, covered with rows upon rows of white crosses, I found my beloved brother, Aaron ...

GOLD STAR MOTHER. ... what greater sacrifice can a woman make than to give her precious sons, brothers and husbands for her country ...

BETSY. ... on the first snowy day in December Jack arrived home, his coffin draped in an American Flag. The boys and I met the train; I was wearing my new dress ...

VIETNAM NURSE. ... GET DOWN, GET DOWN ... nothing has changed ...

SPECIALIST FOURTH CLASS DELANEY. ... we serve; we are abused; we come home — we fight the demons ...

VIETNAM MARINE. ... the fog cleared and everything was peaceful ... just like eating your tiramisu, Ma — food I'll share with the angels ...

Ma, don't cry.

(A moment of silence as lights fade to black. A song like For What It's Worth *comes up full for curtain call and fades into a song like* How did I Get Here *as audience leaves the theatre.)*

SUGGESTED LIST OF SONGS[*]

String of Pearls by Glen Miller
For What It's Worth by Buffalo Springfield
On a Wing and a Prayer
Big Gun performed by ICE-T
White Christmas by Irving Berlin performed by Bing Crosby
God Bless America performed by Kate Smith
Boogie Woogie Bugle Boy performed by Andrew Sisters
Over There performed by Jack Benny
Praise the Lord and Pass the Ammunition performed by The Merry Macs
Wayward Wind performed by Gogi Grant
IRAQ TMIZ
Tell the Truth performed by Mos Def
Oh Johnny performed by The Andrew Sisters
The Unknown Soldier performed by The Doors

LIST OF SOUND CLIPS USED IN WOMEN IN WAR

President Obama State of the Union Address Feb 22, 2009- "Yes We Can"
Katie Couric/Tom Brokaw speaking on 9/11-NBC Nightly News
It's That Man Again from the Army Special Report
Edward R. Murrow's *I Can Hear It Now*
D-Day Speech by Dwight D. Eisenhower
Fibber McGee and Molly Show radio show
Ma Perkins radio show

---

[*]Please see Music Use Note on Page 3

ADDITIONAL MONOLOGUES
To Accompany *Women and War*

Playwright's Note: The following monologues are for use as research into the characters that appear in the published script or as additional work to be used outside of the production of the play. Actors may use these monologues for classroom work or as audition pieces for productions of the play. The monologues may be inserted into the play, as indicated in the script, if producers wish to lengthen the running time of the play. The section titled "Three Soldiers" is not a monologue but might be used as an insert into the script if the cast includes three or more male actors. **Additional changes to the script must be approved by the playwright.**

EMILY

[Part I]

I admit I am bit of a bookworm and I thrive on research. When I was in college I took a course in military history of the United States and I have been fascinated by the subject ever since. Doing research on the Civil War, I came across a story about a young woman. Her name was Emily. Oh, not to confuse you, I am Emily too — Emily Jordan. I don't know Emily's last name, the only other thing was that she grew up on Brooklyn, like myself. Here, let me read in part what I found out about Emily.

"It was sometime during 1863, a young 19 year old woman named Emily ran away from home, disguised herself as a boy, and joined the Grand Army drum corps as a soldier. Emily was sent to Tennessee and during the struggle for Chattanooga, a mine ball pierced the side of the girl. Her wound was mortal; her gender was revealed. As she lay dying, she dictated a telegram to her father in Brooklyn, New York. It read, "Forgive your dying daughter. I have but a few moments to live. My native soil drinks my blood. I expected to deliver my country, but the fates would not have it so. I am content to die. Pray forgive me Emily.""

Emily inspired me to do further research about American women and their roles in war. So I went back to an earlier war, the first American war. The Revolutionary War. Surely women had a role there as well. I found that the Revolution, like all wars that followed, disrupted life for the American woman. The Emilys of that war either stayed at home to manage their homes alone or chose to go with their husbands to war. They were commonly known as "camp followers." Although this term has come to be synonymous with ladies of the night, the camp followers of the American Revolution were generally married women — some with children — following their men from battleground to battleground, doing the cooking, doing the laundry, and serving as nurses to their husbands and other soldiers. There were other Emilys who dressed as men, fought in the war and were recognized as part of the military. They received rations — half for themselves and one quarter for their children — and, most importantly, were subject to military discipline.

Women faced the danger of rape whether they were with the troops or left behind. In 1779 the Connecticut towns of New Haven and Fairfield were raided. Women were brutalized and raped there, and in places like Staten Island and in New Jersey when they were occupied in the fall and winter of 1776. American women were kidnapped and held in Newark by British troops who went "about the town by night, entering houses and openly inquiring for women."

After the Battle of Gettysburg, in July of 1863, the bodies of two women in Confederate uniforms were discovered. There are other accounts of women who died in the great Civil War; the War between the States.

Ellen May Tower of Byron, Michigan was the first U.S. Army nurse to die on foreign soil. She succumbed to typhoid fever in Puerto Rico during the Spanish-American

War, and was the first women to receive a military funeral in Michigan.

In 1944 the 'risk rule' was rescinded allowing women to take jobs where they were put in direct lines of fire. Today the only jobs off limits to women are in submarines, the infantry, and Special Operation Forces.

Thirteen women died in the Gulf War and in that brief war two women were taken POW. One, after her release, reported that she was tortured and sexually abused by her Iraqi captors."

Nothing seems to have changed — history keeps repeating itself.

AXIS SALLY

This is Berlin calling. Berlin calling American mothers and wives. When Berlin calls it pays to listen. It pays to listen to what Sally has to say.

I am an American girl sitting at the microphone with a few words of truth to the American women back home.

There is a reason why I am in Berlin; a good reason why I am transmitting to you from Germany. A reason why I am not with you, in sewing bees, knitting socks for our boys overseas.

That reason is I am not on the side of President Roosevelt and his Jewish friends. I have been brought up to be a 100 percent American girl. So I say damn Roosevelt! Damn all Jews who made this war possible. I love America, but I do not love Roosevelt and all his kike boyfriends.

Conscious of everything American, conscious of our friends, conscious of our enemies — and our enemies are precisely those who are fighting against the Germans today. In case you don't know it, fighting against America, too. A defeat for Germany would be a defeat for America. I want to have a heart-to-heart to talk with you. I am convinced that it is the truth and I feel that the truth will win — and besides that, you know I am in constant touch with your men over here who have been imprisoned in Germany as prisoners of war, and I know you would like to hear from them from time to time, and I'll do my best to transmit that to you just as I plan.

I will put all the energy I can into these few moments I have with you each week, to try to get you to see the light of day, and to get you to realize that you are on the wrong side of the fence.

Now before we hear some music, here is a message for Sgt. Robert Smith: 'Sgt. Do you remember Bill Jones, the guy with the flashy convertible who always had an eye for your wife, Annabelle? Well, they have been seen together frequently over the past few months, and *(gasp)* he moved in with her.' *(Sigh)* Let's take a break here and listen to some Glen Miller.

DOUGHNUT GAL

[Part I]

I know you've heard of the USO Girls, the gals that drove club mobiles during the war. We called 'em "kitchens on wheels" from which we served freshly cooked doughnuts and fresh, steaming hot coffee. Well, I called myself a 'doughnut gal.' Molly is my name. From down south Alabama.

We gals of the USO had to be at least twenty-five years old and college educated. So, guess what, we used our higher education to drive near the front lines in northern France in a two-ton army truck equipped with doughnut machines and big coffee urns. Did you know that a greater percentage of USO Girls — Doughnut Gals — were killed in action in the European Theatre than gals from any of the other women's services? Put that in your record book, Uncle Sam.

Another thing, we weren't in the army, but we were given officer status just in case we were captured and put in prisoner camps, so we would be treated with more respect.

Did the brass really think that our enemies would treat any prisoner with respect? Much less a bunch of gals making doughnuts. The krauts would probably put us to work in the kitchens making strudel — strudel-doodle, strudel-doodle. *(She mimics Hitler, putting one finger under her nose and the other hand in the "heil" salute position.)* Ha! Ha!

My doughnut companion, Alice Percy — well Alice and I would load our old truck — we named her "The Old Ship of Zion" — with sacks of flour, sugar and coffee, and five gallon cans of cooking oil, and hit the road by five every morning. We would take turns driving while the other one was in the back bumping around getting all the ingredients together and the oil hot, so the doughnuts are ready on our first stop. See these biceps? *(She shows her upper arm muscles.)* Got 'em from lifting cans of cooking oil and big sacks of sugar and flour. C'mon, I will take you and you buddies on, two at a time if you like! *(She rolls her sleeve back down.)* Ha! Ha!

By the end of the day we were as greasy as the doughnuts. *(She laughs.)* No need for any beauty lotions for our hair, the oil kept it pretty shiny. After a day 'on the range' as Alice so aptly put it, our blouses and skirts needed degreasing as well.

In 1945 Alice and I split up, she was sent to Le Harve, and I — well lucky me — I was sent to England where my doughnut days continued and my jitterbugging days began. There was this very large, empty warehouse building where the boys would assemble waiting for their next assignments. There was lots of music, and the boys loved to jitterbug and since I knew a few steps of my own, I went from being a 'doughnut girl' to being a 'jitterbug girl' without blinking an eye. Give 'em some coffee and hot doughnuts, and jitter they would. And oh boy, could those boys jitterbug.

LOS ALAMOS WIFE

In the summer of 1972 I was traveling in Japan alone. Tom had died the year before and all the boys were grown and had families of their own. I took a side trip to Hiroshima and I stood looking up at the memorial. I don't know what I expected to feel. To this day I still don't know how I felt standing there. Confused and empty, I suppose. But then a horrible feeling of guilt began to creep up from the soles of my feet and into my heart. My heart started beating rapidly and as if in fear — or was it anger — I turned and ran back to my hotel room — I booked a return flight home.

Tom was finishing up as a teaching assistant after completing his PhD in Chemical Engineering at MIT in 1943 when one of his professors called him in for a chat. When he got home that night he told me to pack, that we were leaving MIT and Boston. I asked him where we were going and all he would say was "out West." Now let me tell you, "out West," is a mighty big place, but when I tried to get him to be more specific he refused to discuss the matter further. He did state, profoundly, "You can ask me all the questions you want, but I can not give you any answers. So, honey, just come along for the ride."

We packed up our '39 Ford coupe with all our belongings which included a pop-up toaster, an electric roaster and coffee peculator — wedding gifts all — and every stitch of clothing plus a few things I bought at the last minute that I assumed would be climate-appropriate out there, "out West."

The drive across the country was uneventful and we landed, in more ways than one, in a mysterious gated compound on a high mesa called Los Alamos in New Mexico. It had once been a school for boys. Childless, we were assigned a one-bedroom apartment in a complex of houses that I swear had walls as thin as paper. I was instructed by Tom to always talk in a whisper and if I played the radio during the day I was to make sure the volume was kept as low as possible. And above all, I was not to ask questions about why we were there, of him or anyone else.

[Part II]

So there I sat in Los Alamos with my toaster, roaster, and peculator with little to do but be quiet and try to keep busy. The apartment was equipped with a wood-burning stove so my electrical appliances came in very handy, that is — when there was electricity. I was assigned an Indian maid for one-half a day each week — the rest of the time I managed to keep the small apartment clear of coal dust by myself.

Tom worked every day, sometimes 10 or 12 hours or more. Our social life consisted of getting together with other young couples, some with children, and sharing meals, going to the movie house on the complex, and occasionally a dance on the weekends. So, you guessed it, before I could say the word "nuclear," a word, by the way, I was absolutely never to utter, I became pregnant. They said that eight babies were born in Los Alamos the first year, but ten were born each month after that. You might say it was a baby boom! Our new baby catapulted us up to a two-bedroom apartment, but with no more amenities that we were accustomed to. You had to be pretty far up the food chain to be housed in better quarters like the brick homes, known as bathtub alley, that were exclusively for the top brass; you have heard the names before: Groves, Oppenheimer, Fermi — the names go on and on.

I wanted to name our first-born Adam — Tom was outraged, he said some people might misconstrue that to mean atom, another word that I was forbidden to utter to him or anyone else. Tom Jr. arrived in this no-man's land and his birth certificate states he was born in Post Office Box 1633 — Los Alamos did not exist.

One afternoon Tom came home early and announced that he had a few days off and we were going camping north of Los Alamos. He seemed very nervous; maybe distressed was a better word. So we quickly pulled as much stuff together as we could for the three of us, packed the Ford and off we went. We found a campsite about 50 miles or so from Los Alamos and set up camp. Every time I would begin to ask a question Tom would hold up his hand and say, "STOP!" Tom became so tense that his entire body stiffened and his blue eyes became as cold as steel. We put Tom Jr. to bed in a makeshift tent and sat outside leaning against a tall New Mexico pine. It was a beautiful clear night. Suddenly the heavens were exceptionally brilliant and there was an unexpected glow on the horizon to our south. Tom closed his eyes and wept. He said over and over, "What have I done, oh God, what have I done." When I tried to console him he simply buried himself in his sleeping bag. I could not, I did not, close my eyes until dawn.

I will never forget that night — June 16, 1945, the night I would later learn was called Trinity — less than a month later on August 6, we bombed Hiroshima, and a few days later on August 9, we bined Nagasaki.

I was a part of Los Alamos and the atomic bomb — I wasn't aware, but I was there.

VIETNAM NURSE

[Part I]

I had never been away from home before. I was so young — nobody was ever as young as I was then *(she laughs)* — just a kid out of college. I was a good Catholic girl and like most other Catholic girls, I was given only three pro-fessional options — I could go to a convent, become a nun and be married to the church and live a life of obedience and celibacy — or, option number 2, become a school teacher, teach grammar school, and be a shaper of young minds — or option number three, become a nurse. Well, Florence Nightingale won over Mother Teresa *(a nervous laugh)*. So I became a nurse, not just any nurse, but a nurse in Vietnam.

I have two cousins that returned from Vietnam under the flag, so I knew the chances were that I might not come back alive — but I was determined to come back — either feet first in a box or on my own feet and be proud of my service to the boys who were in need. *(She pauses for a brief second in thought and smiles.)* There is something romantic about the idea. Or is there? I put the question to you.

I had never been away from home before, hell, I was never west of the Sabine River, even though I was a stone's throw from that river separating Texas from Louisiana. My daddy, as I was leaving, took me in his arms and said, "I raised six kids, five of them boys, and now they are men, and here I am sending my only little girl off to war." That was the first and only time I ever saw my daddy cry.

When I got off the helicopter in Nam, the sounds around me were deafening. All I could hear was — and I remember it vividly to this day — "Get down, GET DOWN!" I lowered my head and ran as fast as I could — I was there — I was in it — I was a part of it and it was, and is, a part of me.

My supervising nurse looked at me after I had checked in and said, "You just get here?" I said, "yeah", so she said, *(she takes the attitude of a tough broad)* "take my advice sister, either shoot yourself in the foot or go get knocked up, and fast." I did neither.

[Part II]

On my first day in the OR I looked around at a room with rows and rows of beds, every bed full. The heat was so strong you could smell it and the stink of bloody wounds. And, oh yeah, there was the smell of death.

Chaos, the smell — the smell, the yelling — nurses yelling, doctors yelling, GI's yelling — yells and smells — they will always be with me.

I had been an OR nurse in Beaumont, Texas where everything was quiet, clean, sanitized, and orderly — everything in it's place — and all of a sudden I found myself surrounded by chaos — filth and screams. On my first day a body was plopped down on a table in front of me — a boy no more than 18 years old — a bloody sheet over his abdomen and I was ordered to "prep" him — that meant clean his wounds, shave him, if necessary, and Oh, Yeah!, while you are at it remove his severed arm that is hanging by a strip of loose skin.

I can never clear my mind of the sounds, the constant whirling of choppers bringing more boys in on more stretchers — some of them with only a heart beat to prove they were alive. I never got used to the sounds of gunfire. We were hit a lot and we had to protect the injured men — one time under a barrage of fire we had to cover the men with mattresses and when there were no more mattresses, without thinking, I jumped up and covered a boy with my own body — I just jumped on top of him to save his life — I never considered my own.

It seems to never stop — 10 to 20 hours a day — the boys came right off the battle field, filling every bed, to be fixed up enough to either be sent back to the States or die in our keep. There was never a time when you could say, "OK, I've had enough — I'm taking a break — I'm going outside for a smoke or over to the officer's club for a drink." Don't even think about a long cool bath. Forget the makeup — forget having your hair done — forget about yourself — it was not about me, it was about blood, it was about screams of pain, it was about orders being yelled over the sounds of rockets and mortars, it was about those never ending choppers buzzing in and out of the compound and the constant hum of ventilators and the emergency generators. It was about death.

Boys came in all marked up with felt makers, their vital signs written on their bodies and faces, like so many tattoos. *(She composes herself and clears her throat as if lecturing.)* These were our priorities: first, the worse cases with a chance of survival, second, the guys who could wait awhile to be patched up, and third, well *(a break in her voice)* if death is imminent, then death was allowed to take its course.

I'm sorry. *(She wipes her eyes, and another pause.)* When I received my orders to leave Vietnam — a knock came on my door and I was told to prepare to leave. I got up, put on a fresh uniform, packed my bags and went over to the ICU to say goodbye. The ventilators were humming — it was hot and smelled of blood, yelling filled the air — it was exactly as it was the day I arrived. Nothing had changed. What can I say? I am alive and back at home, but only a few of the boys that I nursed are.

HELLO GIRLS

[Part I]

It was bitter cold on the day when I and the other Hello Girls landed in France in 1918. A day that was so much like many days I recall from my childhood in Bangor, Maine. Our stiff new woolen uniforms barely protected us from the brisk whistling wind nor did they keep us from shivering. Hats, scarves and mufflers were caught in the winds — it was as if I was back on the rocky, icy, windy coast of Maine. The turmoil was not just that of rough winter seas crashing on the jagged cost line, but it was the chaos of war.

I had just turned 25 and was an operator for the telephone company in Bangor when I heard that the Army was looking for switchboard operators who spoke French. I immediately applied. My Acadian French background served me well and I considered myself fluent in French. I was one of 223 girls who would be shipped to France. We were sworn into the U.S. Army Signal Corps Telephone Units as soldiers. Think of that, the first women who were not nurses to serve in the Army, and yet, at home we didn't have the right to vote.

We were given officer status, which meant that though we had to purchase our own uniforms, and we would be ruled by the same strict military code of conduct as our male counterparts.

General Pershing had declared that he could not fight the Kaiser's Imperial German Army and the poor French telephone system at the same time. He had wired the Army Chief of Staff in Washington, DC, demanding that the latest in American telephone technology be sent to France along with French-speaking telephone operators.

[Part II]

After arriving in France I was immediately assigned to a station in Chaumont. We were billeted with local families and expected to prepare our own meals. The work was hard — it was rough — it was loud — sometimes the noises of war made it difficult to hear voices from the other end of the line. But we didn't give up; we kept going. We screamed at the top of our lungs in order to be heard through the telephone lines that were tacked to trees and strewn along fence posts. All the girls were screaming into their instruments at the same time. The girls laughed uncontrollably when I told them it sounded like a fox had gotten into the chicken coop. All we had in mind was to aid the boys over there fighting Fritz. The noise continued at night when sirens screamed announcing incoming fire, the sounds of the troops passing — artillery rumbling by — ambulances rumbling over the cobblestones of the narrow streets and past our headquarters to the evacuation hospital in the woods just out of town. The telephone lines would go out because of bombs and sometimes thunderstorms. The night sky would light up with the red and yellow glow from explosions in the distance. It seemed that shrapnel was flying everywhere — some fell just yards from some of our girls. Our boys were taking a toll — there seemed to be graves everywhere — through the fields and up and down the hills — oh, so many crosses! I knew I was doing something important — the excitement — the constant noise kept me going. You know, war has no glory — war has overbearing noise — war has the stench of death. We survived.

I was sent from Chaumont to Souilly to reinforce the number of girls there. Conditions were awful. The weather was cold and it rained constantly and there was mud everywhere. Our boots and the bottom of our skirts were caked with mud. The work became harder and harder; we worked in a steamy room and our nerves became vessels of thin crystal that might explode at any moment. We persevered; we kept control. In Souilly, the morning of November 11th, we handled heavier than usual voice traffic until the noises of war ceased. I remember that day well; it was another blustery cold day in November.

There was a band concert that night in the village square. We took the cold icy air into our lungs and breathed out and saw our breaths float into the night's starry sky as the band played every American song they knew. The noises of war had suddenly turned into the French singing *La Marseillaise* mingled with the wonderful sounds of *Alexander's Ragtime Band.*

But we weren't heroes; no, we were just "Hello Girls."

When the "Hello Girls" returned to the States we were told that we were no longer "sworn in" members of the Army. Only men could be sworn in. After failing to persuade Congress in 1930 to recognize us as full-fledged members of the military, and more than fifty bills granting veteran status to the "Hello Girls" were introduced in Congress. Finally in 1978 we succeeded. Congress passed a bill to recognize the 223 women as veterans. Only a handful of us were still alive.

CAMP FOLLOWER

[Part I]

My name is Barbara Berry, my friends call me Babs, and I am a "camp follower." Now don't get your drawers in a twist — most people, when they hear the words "camp follower" immediately think it applies to the bad girls, you know, the girls who hang around army camps selling their pleasures to homesick young men away from home. You can rest assured I am not one of those kinda gals. Nope. I am a married woman. Barry and I were married two weeks before he was drafted and got his marching papers. You would love Barry too, if you met him — even on the street, if he passed you, he would say hello and ask about your mom — even though he never met you — or your mom. I am more of a shy person myself, but I do smile at strangers now. Barry has at least taught me that.

After basic training Barry was sent down to Louisiana, to Camp Claiborne in the middle of a piney woods crawling with snakes. Ooooooh! I took the first Southern Trailways bus out of Lawton, Oklahoma to this town, Alexandria, known as "Alec" to the natives. When I arrived, Barry met me at the Trailways bus depot on Third Street.

[Part II]

We needed a place to stay. The few hotels were all booked, so we immediately began walking, going from house-to-house, knocking on doors, and ringing doorbells. After many hours of, "Sorry buddy, but we don't have no spare rooms to rent. Sorry Ma'am!" We passed this lady and her three young children sitting on a swing in a front yard. When Barry asked her if she had a room to rent she told us that her husband was in the hospital and she had little income to pay the rent and feed the kids. She said she only had four rooms in her house and no inside facilities, except running water in the kitchen. But, she said, if that was all right with us maybe she could put up a bed — if we could find one ourselves — in the living room. So Barry went out on a mission to find a bed, I stayed behind and played with the kids and their dog. By the way the dog could jump rope almost as good as the kids. Barry found an old davenport at a used furniture store not far from the house and with the help of some of his army buddies, carried it down the gravel road to the little house. Mrs. C, as I called her, also allowed us kitchen privileges. We were so lucky to find Mrs. C early on. After we moved in there were army men begging just to rent the garage, but since it had a dirt floor and no plumbing at all she would not agree.

Later, she moved herself into the back bedroom with her three children and rented her bedroom to another couple, Sally and Joe Malone from up north — true Yankees they were. They talked funny and I guess we did too, being Oakies in the Louisiana bayous. One day Mrs. C told me that her landlord, old Mr. Sweeny — who lived two houses down — gave her notice that she had to vacate the house because she was running a house of ill repute. Well, he put it more bluntly she said, quote, "You and yer kids gotta move — you ain't running no whore house on my property!" So she told me and Sally, "Gals get your husbands and your marriage licenses ready, we are going to court." Ms. C couldn't afford a lawyer, so she pleaded her case herself, and won! So we stayed and became known as Mrs. C's "Camp Followers." Now I tell you, Madam C was a saint to us, and no way was she any other kind of Madam. She took care of me and Sally like we were two of her own kids. *(She looks up as if to thank the heavens.)* Thanks, Mrs. C.

WESTERN UNION GIRL

Sometimes I come to the icebox, open the door, and just stand there, wondering what it was that I came here for. Memory is a funny thing at my age. "Madge", I say to myself, "what's come over you?" Then I hear the tick-tock-tick of the old regulator on the wall, and I am back one day in June, 1944.

As a girl I worked after school and during the summer at Culpepper's Drug Store. I had one more year in school, and it was summer break so I spent most of my days helping Mrs. Culpepper with the morning coffee and biscuits. You see, most of the men of Baylor, old Judge Sullivan, Doc Levy — he delivered Billie, my youngest brother, me and Aaron, my older brother — Sheriff McCoy, the mayor and other business men would gather at Culpepper's for their morning coffee and Mrs. Culpepper's biscuits. I remember to this day how Doc Levy would holler to Mrs.

Culpepper, "put a rock on my biscuit so's it won't float off the plate." Mrs. Culpepper's biscuits were that light. After many years he would just clear his throat and say, "One biscuit and one rock, Maude. Please!", and laughter would fill the store and the morning and everybody would go about their day feeling good. But there was this day in June that wasn't so good.

You see, most of the boys and young men in Baylor went from high school right to work on their family's farm or in the mills; few if any, ever went away to college. So for a few extra dollars in their pockets they would join the National Guard spending one night a month playing soldier and having fun and for a week each year they would 'train' in the western part of the state. Aaron, my older brother, joined the Guard as soon as he was old enough. When the war began in Europe, the entire unit was called into active duty and was eventually sent to England to wait for orders to cross the channel to fight Hitler.

Part of my job was to turn on the Western Union machine and connect with Lexington in case there were telegrams to be received and delivered. That morning, I went into the little back room — well it wasn't really a room, just a cubical, I think they would call it today — and switched on the teletype machine and when it warmed up I typed "Good Morning, go ahead. Baylor." And the reply came "Good Morning. Lexington. We have casualties." And the machine began to sputter and click, click, click, shooting out tape like I had ever seen before.

It was June 6, 1944 when our boys were sent to that beach in France the army called Omaha. Heroes all. Over 10,000 lost their lives and were buried on the bluff overlooking the sea — some were eventually sent home in boxes draped with the American flag.

Click, click, click, the tape just kept coming. I did my best to put the tape in the tank of water and with my thimble and ruler stripped it onto the yellow Western Union stationery. "The Secretary of War desires me to express my feeling of regret ..." click, click, click. Another yellow piece of paper, another address, another name, another regret. I pasted, and I pasted. Click, click, click — 'regret' John Seers — click, 'regret' Albert Staulings — click, 'regret' Andy Barrow — click, click, click.

My younger brother, Billie, rode up on his old Montgomery-Ward bicycle — handed down from Aaron — there was six years difference in their ages, with me in the middle. He leaned it against the fire hydrant in front of Culpepper's that morning. Billie helped me out by delivering the telegram whenever there was one. That day there was more than he could handle, a young boy on his bike up and down the hills of Baylor, the entire county, and out to the farms all around. By this time the men had left the coffee shop, so I called Sheriff McCoy to say that I needed help. He organized a group of local men with cars or trucks and they delivered the telegrams. Click — click — click. "Regrets" Bobby Barnes ... 'regret' Dudley Dickerson ... 'regrets' Larry Holloway — click — click — click.

All in all, there were more telegrams than I can remember. As lunchtime approached I was pretty much in a daze and then — click — click — click ... "It is with profound regret that I ... click ... Aaron MacAlister," my dear brother ...

In 1994 on the fiftieth anniversary of D-Day, 'the longest day' they called it, I went to France and among the rows and rows of white marble crosses, on a bluff overlooking the sea, I found my beloved brother, Aaron.

Now, what was it that I came to the icebox for? Oh yeah, the milk.

THREE SOLDIERS' LETTERS TO THEIR MOMS

SOLDIER #1. Vietnam, March 30, 1971

SOLDIER #2. Kuwait, February 25, 1991

SOLDIER #3. Korea, December 7, 1953

ALL SOLDIERS. Dear Mom,

SOLDIER #1. I hate to tell you this Mom, but we got our butts kicked badly yesterday. The dinks fired more than 150 rounds of mortar and hit us with even more machine gun fire.

SOLDIER #2. There is sand everywhere — they are calling it Desert Storm. I'm OK Mom, but some of my buddies are dead.

SOLDIER #3. We were sent to Chu Lai to regroup and re-supply. Fresh troops are coming in to replace the men we lost. I'm OK — the enemy didn't see me.

SOLDIER #1. Mom the total for the battle was 45 dead, 63 wounded, plus another 15 missing in action which means they were blown to bits and pieces and can't be identified. We counted only 13 North Vietnamese dead on the battlefield.

SOLDIER #2. Don't worry about me, Mom.

SOLDIER #3. I wasn't hurt so I won't be getting another purple heart.

SOLDIER #2. It is sheer hell, the windstorms and the sand.

SOLDIER #3. Many of our men survived because they went limp and played dead. The dinks then stripped the dead and those playing dead of their watches, rings and other personal valuables. Some even took their dog tags — as souvenirs I guess. One buddy, Mike, was shot in his chest and legs, groaned when a dink kicked him to see if he was alive. My buddy John saw a dink beat one of our men in the head with a rock till he died.

I patched a few guys up and played dead, too. Boys had legs and arms blown off and I saw so many die of just shock. I curse this war. Please don't worry — I'm AOK Mom, but scared I will not have the courage to go out in the bush again.

SOLDIER #1. The guys that are left are messed up. I hear that 45 new troops will join us soon and we will have to train them before they go to battle.

SOLDIER #3. Mom, please don't worry, OK?

SOLDIER #2. The news journalists and film crews are embedded with us now Mom. But I believe that they are not telling the truth to the folks back home. Between the wind and the sand they seem to be looking through rose-colored glasses. The horrors, the hardships, the total disbelief that we are living through this hell does not seem to impress them. So don't believe all you see on TV or read in the newspapers and magazines. We are in a living hell. We lost our first female soldier yesterday — she was only a supply officer, but still — *(pause)* Women and War!

SOLDIER #3. I guess it is not a time to bitch, I can't see the truth being told in the U.S. because the war over here is ended. Bull Shit. Sorry about the language Mom. A lot of men get killed and only a small number is reported. Mom, I'm sick of this shit. All I want is to get the hell out of here as soon as possible. It is not just the gooks, I walked in on two GIs raping a young girl the other day, it seems that this war is bringing out the ugly sides of Americans here — Women and War!

SOLDIER #1. Take care, Mom …

SOLDIER #2. … and remember I love you Mom so don't worry …

SOLDIER #3. I'll come home soon Mom.

SOLDIER #1. It's late and I'm OK Mom.

SOLDIER #2. I need some sleep Mom.

SOLDIER #3. I need to get drunk and then sleep.

ALL SOLDIERS. Love, your son.

OTHER TITLES AVAILABLE FROM BAKER'S PLAYS

FREEDOM FIRES

Lucile McIntyre

*4m, 3f, + extras, flexible casting / Drama High School/
Community Theatre / Unit set*

Jesse's leadership in Iraq began with her standing up to bullies in grade school. The same toughness that forced Jesse to defeat bullies early in life appears again on a battlefield far from home. Courage, beliefs, fear, and love of mankind are all called into play. The gritty American soldiers of past wars also fight for Jesse's survival in these moments when Jessie may live or die. The same respect for preparation that brought Jesse a full college scholarship for softball earlier has brought her fellow soldiers the ability to assist in miracles in an unforeseen place. Teamwork, inner strength, and determination propel this powerful glimpse of heroism.

With a playing time that allows inclusion in major high school and community play competitions, powerful monologues for males and females, easy set and props, this script can bring out the best in actors and in audiences.

OTHER TITLES AVAILABLE FROM BAKER'S PLAYS

BUSINESS AS USUAL

Jean Battlo

Dramatic Comedy / 3m, 5f / Interior

Set in Southern West Virginia in the 1990's when the last coal mines were closing, *Business as Usual* is a hilarious slice of human comedy based on economic hardship.

Tom Woolwine, who entered the coal mining business at 16, is out of work after the closing of his mine in rural Gary, West Virginia. Despite facing poverty and an uncertain future, Tom does not want a severance check, nor welfare, nor a handout; he wants a job. He and his son Joey have tried everything but to no avail, leaving Tom to wonder "just how far a man will go when he has nowhere to go."

Gran answers that. A true mountain mama with the spirit of "grits", she advises the family: "There's one business that never closes...I'm talking about every funeral home from here to the moon. Now, in the old days, folks didn't go to any such. No, a neighboring friend with good feeling towards you would come and begin to work on the body of your loved one and..."

...Then, the human comedy begins.

This hilarious and touching new play from West Virginian writer Jean Battlo is appropriate for all theatre groups.

OTHER TITLES AVAILABLE FROM BAKER'S PLAYS

THE COOLEY GIRLS

Brad Stephens

Dramatic Comedy

1m, 5f

Three sisters, Rose, Brenda and Harriet Cooley, have been separated since childhood. Now forty-years later one of the sisters, Rose, decides to find her lost siblings and reunite the 'girls'. All of them have secrets to hide, but it is curiosity that finally brings them together for their unexpected reunion. Only when Harriet is forced to admit her most damning secret does this hard bitten and at times humorous play resolves once and for all the bond each shares with the other. Perfect for community stages.